Christmas
PRAYER

A Christmas PRAYER

A cross-country journey in 1850 leads to high mountain danger—and romance.

WANDA E. BRUNSTETTER

New York Times BESTSELLING AUTHOR

SHILOH RUN PRESS

An Imprint of Barbour Publishing, Inc.

A Christmas Prayer © 2014 by Wanda E. Brunstetter

Print ISBN 978-1-68322-657-4

eBook Editions:
Adobe Digital Edition (.epub) 978-1-68322-659-8
Kindle and MobiPocket Edition (.prc) 978-1-68322-658-1

All scripture quotations are taken from the King James Version of the Bible.

This book is a work of fiction. Names, characters, places, and incidents are either products of the author's imagination or used fictitiously. Any similarity to actual people, organizations, and/or events is purely coincidental.

Cover Design: Buffy Cooper
Cover Model Photography: © Richard Brunstetter III, RBIII Studios

Published by Shiloh Run Press, a division of Barbour Publishing, Inc., 1810 Barbour Drive, Uhrichsville, Ohio 44683, www.shilohrunpress.com

Our mission is to inspire the world with the life-changing message of the Bible.

ecpa Member of the
Evangelical Christian
Publishers Association

Printed in Canada.

Continue in prayer, and watch
in the same with thanksgiving.
COLOSSIANS 4:2

Prologue

Independence, Missouri
April 15, 1850

Dear Diary,

Tomorrow Mama and I begin our journey by covered wagon to California— the land of opportunity. We are traveling with Walter Prentice, the man I've agreed to marry. There's gold in California, and Walter plans to open several businesses when we get there. Walter wanted us to be

married before we left New York, but I said I would rather wait until we get settled in California. After all, the dirty, dusty trail is hardly a place for a honeymoon.

When we arrived in Independence four days ago, Walter spent over $1000 for our supplies, plus the covered wagon and three oxen we will need for our nearly 2,000-mile journey west. Our prairie schooner is filled with 200 pounds of flour, 150 pounds of bacon, 10 pounds of coffee, 20 pounds of sugar, and 10 pounds of salt. We also have our basic kitchenware, which consists of a cooking kettle, frying pan, coffeepot, tin plates, cups, knives, and forks. That's in addition to our trunks of clothes and personal items, a few small pieces of furniture, and our bedrolls, tools, and several other things we'll need to survive on this

trip. I'm glad Walter did a little research before traveling. He said it's advised that our supplies should be kept below 2,000 pounds of total weight for the wagon so as not to tire the draft animals.

It will take us anywhere from five to six months to reach our destination, and we'll be traveling with two other wagons, as the larger wagon train we were supposed to join left a week ago, due to the fact that we were all late getting here. Walter says it's nothing to worry about. We'll follow the other wagon train's trail and should be able to catch up with them if nothing goes wrong. I shall pray every day for traveling mercies and look forward to spending this Christmas in a new land.

I'm looking forward to getting to know the people in the two wagons we'll be with.

I haven't met any of them yet, but Walter has. He said a widowed man with two small children owns one of the wagons, and the other wagon is owned by a young single man and his sister. The men will get together in the morning to decide whose wagon will lead and which of them will be in charge of our small group and act as the scout.

Cynthia Cooper stopped writing and sighed. Knowing Walter, he'd probably insist that he be in charge. But then, what did he really know about wilderness travel? While Walter owned two stores in New York City and had a good head when it came to business ventures, as far as Cynthia was aware, he knew nothing about leading a wagon train, even a small one such as theirs.

As she pushed a wayward curl under her

nightcap, a vision of Walter came to mind. At thirty-five, Walter had small ears compared to most men, and his nose was thin and kind of birdlike. Many men his age sported a beard, or at least a mustache, but he chose to be clean shaven. His light brown hair had already begun to recede, although his side-whiskers were thick. Walter's most outstanding feature was his closely set brown eyes. Sometimes when he looked at Cynthia in a certain way, she felt as if he could see right into her soul and know what she was thinking. When Walter studied Cynthia in that manner, she shivered, and not in a good way.

Cynthia didn't think Walter was ugly. He just wasn't the handsome man she'd dreamed of marrying; not to mention that he was fifteen years older than her. Walter seemed more like an uncle or big brother, if she had one, that is. Unfortunately, Cynthia was an only child.

Cynthia hadn't agreed to become Walter's wife because she loved him. She would become Mrs. Walter Prentice so she and Mama would be taken care of financially. Truthfully, she was doing it mostly for Mama's sake. When Papa died from an unexpected illness six months ago, they'd been left almost penniless. Unbeknownst to Cynthia and her mother, Papa had taken part in a business venture that went sour, and he'd used up all their savings. In hindsight, they realized the stress from all that may have been what killed him, but it was one of those things they'd never know for sure.

Since Papa's death, poor Mama had been forced to take in boarders in order to put food on their table. Struggling for six months might not seem very long, but it was difficult for a woman who'd been used to the finer things in life. Walter, whom they'd met at a social function

before Papa's untimely death, had saved the day when he'd asked Cynthia to marry him.

Pulling her gaze back to the journal, Cynthia finished her entry:

I'm looking forward to our trip to California for the adventure of going someplace I haven't been before. It will be exciting to see new things along the way, and good to start over. It was always Papa's dream to see the West, so I'm sure he would be happy to know Mama and I have the opportunity to make this trek. My only regret is that Papa isn't going with us.

Cynthia set her pen and paper aside and placed one hand against her chest. *Oh Papa, I miss you so much. No matter where I go, you'll always be here in my heart.*

Chapter 1

Three days out of Independence

Papa, I'm tired."

Jack Simpson glanced at his four-year-old son, Alan, slumped on the wagon seat beside his sister. Amelia, who was six, stared straight ahead, seemingly unmindful of her brother. Of course, Jack's daughter had been unresponsive to most things since she'd

witnessed her mother's tragic death six months ago. Jack's precious wife, Mary, had been crossing the street in their hometown of Cedar Rapids, Iowa, and was struck down by a team of runaway horses pulling a supply wagon. Clem Jones, the owner of the wagon, hadn't tied the horses securely enough. Poor little Amelia, waiting across the street with her grandma, had watched in horror as her mother was knocked to the ground and trampled to death. Since that time, the child had not uttered a word.

Jack, struggling with his own grief plus trying to keep some sense of normalcy in his children's lives, could only hope this trip west might be the turning point for Amelia. There was no doubt that Alan was excited about the trip and a new place to live. The boy had been bursting at the seams waiting to head west ever since Jack first mentioned the trip to his

children. Truth was, Jack needed the change too and looked forward to joining his brother, Dan, already in California, where he'd established a cattle ranch.

Being a hog farmer, Jack knew a thing or two about pigs, but not much concerning the business of raising cattle. He was eager to learn though and would do his best to help Dan make a go of things. Jack just needed to get his little family and all their belongings safely to their destination.

"Papa, I'm tired," Alan repeated, bumping Jack's arm as he guided their team of oxen down the trail. "Can't them ox move faster?"

"Why don't ya crawl in the back and lie down?" Jack suggested. "Amelia, you can go too if you're tired. It shouldn't be much longer before we stop to make camp."

Alan scrambled over the seat and into the

back of their wagon, but Amelia, her long auburn locks moving slightly as she shook her head, remained seated.

Will my little girl ever speak to me again? Jack wondered as he held on to the reins, bringing up the rear of their three-wagon train. He drew in a deep breath, trying to focus on the wagon ahead driven by a stuffy city dweller from New York who thought he knew a lot about everything but probably knew very little about roughing it. The man's name was Walter Prentice, and his traveling companions were a woman named Mable and her daughter, Cynthia, who was Walter's fiancée. Jack had only spoken to Cynthia briefly, but she seemed nice enough. She was pretty too, and from the way she talked, Jack figured she didn't know much about roughing it either. It would be a miracle if this refined group ahead of him made it to California at all. Thank goodness, back in

Independence when the men drew names to see who would lead out, the man in the first wagon got the luck of the draw. Jack was pretty sure Cole Edwards knew a lot more about driving a team of oxen than Walter Prentice did.

Cole had never been one to take the easy way out, and he knew heading to California in search of gold wasn't going to be easy. But he was tired of the long hours he put in at his blacksmith's shop in Kutztown, Pennsylvania, and the money he hoped to make in the gold mines near Sutter's Mill would make the trip worth every mile and inconvenience. If he didn't make his fortune in gold, he could always fall back on his blacksmith's trade. He just hoped his sister was up for this trip.

Sitting astride his sturdy quarter horse, Blaze,

Cole glanced back at Virginia, whom he'd nicknamed Ginny when they were children. She sat on the seat of their covered wagon, looking this way and that, as though trying to take in everything on all sides of the trail. Skillfully, she guided their oxen as if she'd been doing it all her life. While Cole's twenty-six-year-old sister wasn't as adventuresome as him, she'd been willing to make this trip, despite negative protests from their parents. Virginia had been teaching school for the past six years and hoped to teach when they got to California. Having been jilted by Clay Summers, the man she'd planned to marry, Virginia told Cole she was ready for a change. In fact, she desperately needed it.

At the age of twenty-four, Cole had courted a few young women but none who'd held his interest or captured his heart. Most women he

knew wanted to settle in to a nice little house with a white picket fence. They weren't seeking adventure the way Cole was, and he wasn't ready to settle in and accept the mediocre comforts in life. He wanted more and aimed to get it.

"You doin' okay, Ginny?" he called. "Do ya need me to take over awhile? I can tie my horse to the back of the wagon."

Smiling, she shook her head. "Thanks, Cole, but I'm fine."

Cole smiled in response. His sister had a determined spirit. She would do fine out West. He wasn't so sure about the two refined ladies in the wagon behind him though. Three days out and they looked exhausted. They obviously weren't used to sitting on a hard bench or walking long hours every day. The fancy fellow accompanying them didn't look much better, although he was trying to put on a brave front

and acted like quite the braggart. Cole wondered if the high-and-mighty Mr. Prentice would be so confident after they had several weeks of traveling under their belts. It was a good thing Walter wasn't trying to lead the way. He'd probably have them lost already.

Glancing upward, Cole noticed dark clouds. No doubt a storm was coming, and he wanted to be sure they were safely camped before it hit. "Ginny, I'm goin' out ahead and find a good spot for the night," he called. Then Cole turned his horse around and went back to tell those in the other wagons.

"Are you okay, Mama?" Cynthia asked, concerned when she noticed lines of fatigue on her mother's face. "You look awfully tired."

"Mable is fine, and so am I." Walter spoke up before Cynthia's mother had a chance to respond. "We have a long journey ahead of us, and we need to toughen up. Otherwise, we won't make it to California. We haven't been on the trail a week yet and have hundreds of miles ahead of us."

"That may be true, but I believe my mother can speak for herself." Cynthia patted her mother's hand affectionately.

"I'm fine, dear," Mama replied, reaching up to touch the bun at the back of her head. "No need to worry about me. It takes some time getting used to sitting on this hard bench, and walking is just as uncomfortable. But I'll make it—we all will."

Cynthia smiled. Her mother might be slender and petite, but she had a determined spirit. Mama's brown hair and eyes were accentuated by her oval face, thick dark eyebrows, and thin lips. Except for their slender build, Cynthia

and Mama looked nothing alike. Cynthia had inherited her father's curly auburn hair and green eyes. Even the two dimples in her right cheek came from Papa.

Looking back at Mama, Cynthia noted that even at the age of forty-five, her mother was still an attractive woman. It was unlikely she would ever marry again. Mama had been deeply in love with Papa and said that no one could take his place. That's what Cynthia had always wished for too, but it seemed she'd never know the kind of love her mother and father had.

It doesn't matter whether Mama remarries or not, Cynthia thought. *Once Walter and I are married, Mama won't have to worry about anything, for she'll be well taken care of.*

Cynthia glanced at Walter wiping some dust from his eyes with his clean, crisp, monogrammed handkerchief. His expression was one

of determination. She knew with a certainty that his desperation to get to California was about the money he planned to make. She guessed she couldn't blame him for that. After all, everyone needed money these days—some just wanted it more than others. Walter was one of those who measured people by their wealth and social standing.

Cole Edwards, the man who was leading their little group, was also after money; only his would be earned by the sweat of his brow as he searched for gold. That wasn't to say Walter was lazy; he just didn't work as hard physically as some men she knew. Walter had a good head for business though.

Just then, Cole pulled his horse alongside their flat-bedded wagon made of hardwood and covered with canvas like the others. "Just wanted to let you folks know that I'm ridin' up

ahead to find a good place to take shelter for the night. It'll be dark soon, and there's a storm brewin'."

"It doesn't look as if a storm is coming," Walter said.

"Take a closer look. See those clouds?" Cole looked at Walter with piercing blue eyes, as if daring him to question his decision. "If we get caught out here in the pouring rain, the trail will be muddy, and it'll bog us down. It doesn't take much for these wagon wheels to get stuck in the mud. Best to stop for the night and hope the rain lets up."

"What are we supposed to do while you're looking for a good place to stop?" Walter questioned.

"Keep moving—following the ruts in the trail made by wagons that have gone before us." Cole glanced at Cynthia and gave a nod. "You

and your mother doin' okay?"

"They're fine," Walter answered before Cynthia could open her mouth. "Even if they weren't, it's my business, not yours."

"Walter, I'm sure Mr. Edwards is concerned for the welfare of everyone," Mama intervened.

Cole gave a nod, reaching under his hat and pulling his fingers through the ends of his coal-black hair. He really was a good-looking young man. But then, so was Jack.

Walter said nothing, just gripped the reins a little tighter, making the veins on his hands stick out.

"I'll tell Jack Simpson where I'm goin', and then I'm off," Cole said. He tipped his hat and rode quickly away.

They rode in silence for a while, until rain-drops began to fall. Mama looked over at Walter and said, "I guess Mr. Edwards was right."

Walter grunted.

Cynthia hid a smile behind her hand. For some reason, she was glad Cole had been right about the weather. No man should think he was always right. *And Mama, she sure isn't afraid to stand up to Walter. Maybe I ought to take a lesson from her.*

Chapter 2

South fork of the Platte River

Dear Diary,

We've been on the trail a week already, but it feels more like a month to me. The rain we had awhile back caused our wagons to bog down in the mud. I feel like I'll never be clean again, not to mention my poor dresses with mud-stained hems. What

I wouldn't give right now for a warm tub to soak in.

No sign of the bigger wagon train yet. I hope we're not going the wrong way and will miss them. But Cole insists we're on the right trail, so we have to trust him.

We take turns walking when we're tired of sitting, and riding in the bumpy wagon when we're tired of walking.

I feel sorry for Jack Simpson. His children are too young to drive the wagon and too little to walk very far without their legs giving out. Mama and I have begun taking turns riding in Jack's wagon with the children, driving his team of oxen so Jack can walk awhile each day and stretch his legs. Little brown-haired Alan looks a lot like his father, and he certainly is a chatterbox. But Amelia doesn't speak at all.

Jack explained that she's been like that since she witnessed her mother's death. Poor little thing. I wonder if she'll ever get her voice back. I've begun praying for her.

Cynthia stopped writing and looked up as Cole hollered that it was time to go. With regret, she put her journal away and joined her mother on the seat of their wagon. Every day on the trail seemed like the one before. They got up before daybreak, and while the men rounded up the livestock, the women cooked breakfast over an open fire. After the meal, it was time to head down the trail.

Some days they stopped to rest for an hour or two; then they'd continue on their journey until early evening. At night they pulled the wagons close together for protection. The men took care of the livestock, while the women

cooked the evening meal. After they ate, they'd often gather around the fire to sing songs and tell stories. This helped pass the time and gave them a chance to get better acquainted. The women and children slept inside the wagons, but Cole, Jack, and Walter slept under the wagons or in a makeshift tent, depending on the weather. It made Cynthia feel safer, knowing they were out there where they could be alerted to danger.

Cynthia shivered. At least they hadn't seen any Indians yet. If and when they did, she hoped they would be friendly natives and there'd be no trouble. From what Walter had been told, fewer people died from Indian attacks than from mishaps or illness along the way.

"What do you write in that book of yours?" Walter asked as he took up the reins.

"Oh, just the things we see and do on our daily journey," Cynthia replied. "I've been

writing since I was fifteen."

Walter shrugged. "If it makes you happy, it's a good thing. Maybe someday you can read me what you've written about our trip."

Cynthia cringed. Since she'd written about her lack of interest in Walter, she wasn't about to let him know what was in her diary.

He leaned closer to Cynthia—so close she could feel his warm breath blowing gently on her cheek. "You look lovely this morning, my dear," he whispered.

Her face heated. "I thank you for the compliment, but I certainly don't feel lovely," she said. "I feel dirty from all the trail dust, and even though I wash every evening and morning, I feel unkempt."

"You'll feel better once we get to California," he said, letting go of the reins with one hand and clasping her hand. "After I get my new

businesses going, you'll be the finest dressed woman in all of California."

Cynthia forced a smile. She didn't care about being the finest-dressed woman. All she wanted was to be happily married and see that her mother's needs were met. Cynthia wasn't sure if she would be happy married to Walter, but at least Mama would be taken care of.

"Papa, I'm hungry," Alan complained, squirming on the wooden seat beside his father.

Jack relaxed his hold on the reins, reached into his shirt pocket, and pulled out a piece of peppermint candy. "We won't be stoppin' to eat for a good while yet, so you can suck on this for now." He handed it to Alan. "Just be careful to suck it slowly, and whatever ya do, don't swallow the candy."

Alan popped the candy in his mouth and

grinned up at his dad. "Yum."

Jack smiled and took another piece from his pocket. It was all he had left from what he'd purchased before they'd departed Independence. There was no doubt about it—his son had a sweet tooth. "You want this?" he asked, holding out the last piece of candy to Amelia.

She shook her head.

Jack couldn't believe Amelia didn't want a piece of candy. Was there nothing that could get through to his daughter? He wouldn't force her to take the treat. He just needed to be patient and keep trying to get her to talk.

"Can I have the candy?" Alan asked, tugging on his father's arm.

"Thought maybe I'd eat it," Jack replied with a grin.

Alan's bottom lip protruded. "Please, Papa. I'll save it for later."

Jack looked at Amelia again. "Are ya sure you don't want the peppermint drop?"

She shook her head again.

"Is it okay if I give it to Alan?"

Amelia gave a slow nod.

Jack handed the candy to Alan.

"Can I drive the wagon?" Alan asked, looking up at Jack with expectancy.

Jack shook his head. "You're not old enough for that yet, son. But someday, when you're a mite bigger, you'll be helpin' me and your uncle Dan on the cattle ranch."

Alan's eyes twinkled. "Can I ride a big horse and chase after cows?"

Jack chuckled. "I don't know how big the horse will be, but yeah, you'll be ridin'."

Seemingly satisfied with that answer, Alan leaned his head against Jack's arm and fell silent.

That evening, as everyone sat around the camp-fire after supper, Cole couldn't help but notice the looks of fatigue on the women's faces. Particularly Cynthia's and Mable's. They'd walked a good deal of the day, while that high-and-mighty gentleman they were traveling with remained in the wagon.

"I don't know about anyone else, but after that bland supper we just ate, I could use something sweet," Walter spoke up. "Think I'll head over to my wagon and get my jar of candy."

"There was nothing wrong with the rabbit stew my sister fixed," Cole was quick to say. "Maybe it didn't measure up to the standards you're used to, but it filled our bellies, and I thought it was right tasty."

"I agree," Jack spoke up. "And since I'm not

much of a cook, I appreciate everything the ladies make for us."

Cole looked at Walter, wondering if he would apologize, but the snobbish man just rose to his feet and reached for Cynthia's hand. "Come, take a walk with me. It's a pleasant evening with a star-studded sky, and we shouldn't waste it."

Like an obedient child, Cynthia went with Walter. As they strolled arm in arm, Cole couldn't help but frown. *Sure can't see what that pretty woman sees in such a stuffy man.*

Cynthia and Walter walked for a bit, making small talk, but as they headed toward Walter's wagon, he stopped, pulled out his gold pocket watch, and checked the time. Just as he was putting the watch back in his pocket, Cynthia caught sight of little Alan peeking into the back of the wagon. Walter must have seen him too

for his face turned red as he shouted, "What do you think you're doing, boy?"

Alan jumped. "N–nothin'. Just wanted to see what ya got there."

"Nothing that pertains to you." Walter gave the boy a little push. "Now go on. . .scat!"

Alan glanced up at Cynthia with a pathetic expression then darted off toward the others still gathered around the campfire.

"That wasn't a nice way to speak to the boy," Cynthia said looking at Walter. "I'm sure you hurt his feelings."

"Well, he shouldn't have been snooping around my wagon. The boy's father ought to keep a closer eye on him."

Cynthia watched as Walter peered into the back of the wagon, presumably making sure nothing was missing. She sighed. "I'm sure Alan meant no harm. He was no doubt curious about

your load of supplies. Little boys are like that, you know. Surely you can remember those days when you were an inquisitive child."

Walter folded his arms and huffed, "More to the point, he was probably looking to steal something from me."

"I doubt that. I mean, what do you have that a little boy would want to take?"

Walter shrugged, pulling on the lapels of his jacket. He took out his pocket watch once more to check the time. "It could be anything. A child like that with no mother to teach him right from wrong could take things just for the fun of stealing. But everything seems to be in place. That rascal is lucky this time."

Cynthia didn't argue with Walter. It was obvious that he had made up his mind. She did wonder though what kind of father he would make. Would he be so strict with their children

that they wouldn't have any fun? Worse yet, would his harsh tone and expectations cause them to be afraid? Was Walter Prentice the kind of man she should marry? She'd noticed that he did do some peculiar things, like just now, checking the time when he'd looked at it only moments ago. Perhaps it was something he did without thinking.

Cynthia glanced back at the campfire where Mama sat with the others. *I have to marry Walter,* she told herself. *If I don't, Mama will be disappointed. And what would become of us when we reached California? With no money of our own, we'd be on the streets, begging for food.* She looked up at Walter and forced a smile. *Does he love me, or does he want to marry me for some other reason?*

Chapter 3

Dear Diary,

Three more weeks have passed, and so far we haven't incurred any serious problems along the way. We saw a band of Indians the other day. Fortunately, they followed us for only a few miles, watching from a ridge a good distance away, but they made no move to bother us, which was

an answer to prayer.

Cole told us a few stories as we sat around the campfire last night, about things he'd heard that a few of the Indian tribes had done to some of the earlier pioneers. Horses and food had been stolen. Some people had been killed trying to protect their belongings. I pray every day that God will send His guardian angels to watch over us and take us safely to our destination.

There is still no sign of the wagon train that went ahead of us, and I'm worried. After this much time, we should have caught up to them. Of course, we have been moving rather slowly. Can our three bumpy wagons make it to California with Cole, an inexperienced guide, leading the way?

When Cole rode up to their wagon and said

it was time to get the wagons moving, Cynthia stopped writing and slipped her journal into her reticule. "You holdin' up okay?" he asked.

She smiled. "I'm doing fine."

"What about you?" Cole asked, looking at Cynthia's mother, sitting beside Cynthia on the wagon bench.

Mama sighed while fanning her face with her hand. "If it weren't so hot, I'd be doing a lot better."

Cole lifted the brim of his hat and wiped his wet forehead. "You're right. It is kinda warm, but it's bound to get hotter in the days to come. Just be sure to keep that sunbonnet on your head."

Mama folded her arms and scowled at Cole. "Of course I'll wear my bonnet. I'm not addle-brained, you know."

"Never said you were," Cole shot back as he got down from his horse. "Noticed the lid on

your water barrel is about ready to fall off." After adjusting the lid and making sure the water keg was tied securely to their wagon, he climbed back on the horse. "Water is precious out here on the trail, so make sure someone in your party checks it before we head out each morning."

"Thank you for letting us know." Cynthia smiled when Cole tipped his hat before riding away.

"That man thinks he knows everything," Mama complained. "It's not like he's a real wagon train leader, after all."

Sometimes Mama speaks her mind a little too much, Cynthia thought. *And I wish she could be a little nicer about it.* She decided to let the matter go. The last thing she needed was an argument with Mama today. Truth was, Cynthia's mother had always been quite outspoken, but since Papa died, Mama could be a bit too vocal at

times. Maybe she was angry with Papa for leaving them virtually penniless and struggling to pay the bills on the meager amount she made with a few boarders. Cynthia couldn't blame her for that but felt certain Papa hadn't made poor business decisions on purpose.

"What was Cole complaining about now?" Walter asked, coming from inside the wagon and taking a seat on the bench.

"He said we'd better make sure the water barrel is secure and the lid's on tight before we head out each morning," Cynthia answered.

Walter grunted. "That man sure likes to bark out orders."

"My sentiments exactly," Cynthia's mother agreed.

Cynthia rolled her eyes. It seemed that Walter just liked to complain, and Mama said whatever she thought he wanted to hear. *Is she*

worried that if she doesn't agree with Walter on every little thing, he might not marry me?

"Are you two ladies ready for another boring, tiring day?" Walter asked, taking up the reins.

Cynthia nodded. "Every day sort of blends into the next, doesn't it?"

Walter reached over and gently patted her hand. "It will be worth it when we reach the Promised Land, my dear."

"Promised Land?" Cynthia mentally questioned. *The Bible says the Israelites were headed to the Promised Land, but it took them years and years to get there. I hope our journey takes only months, not years. At the rate we're going, we'll never make it there before Christmas.*

Around noon that day, their travels were halted when a wheel came off Jack's wagon. "Oh great," Jack mumbled. "One more thing to slow us

down." He took the children down from the wagon and told them to stay close while he fixed the wheel. He felt bad about holding all the wagons up, but there was no other choice.

"I'll give you a hand with that," Cole said, stepping up to Jack after securing his horse.

"Thanks, I could use another set of hands."

Cole looked over at Walter who was standing beside his wagon, checking his watch. "Guess we won't be getting any help from him today," he said with a grunt.

"That's okay," Jack responded. "I'm sure we can manage without his help. From what I've seen of Walter so far, he'd probably tell us we were doing it wrong and that his way was better. Not that he would know much about putting a wagon wheel on."

"Ya got that right. Mr. Fancy Pants would probably just get in the way." Cole motioned

to Cynthia, walking beside Virginia, with little Amelia between them. "I'll bet either one of those ladies would be more help fixing your wheel than Walter."

Jack smiled. Cole's sister might try to tackle something like that, but he couldn't picture the pretty little gal from New York lying on the ground, attempting to get the wheel put back in place. Cynthia had other qualities though—besides her beauty. Since the women took turns fixing their meals, Jack had quickly discovered that Cynthia was quite a good cook. She was also good with his children. Amelia, although she still hadn't spoken to anyone, seemed to light up whenever Cynthia talked to her, and that gave Jack some hope.

"Do you need any tools?" Cole asked.

"Nope. Think I have everything I need," Jack responded, going to the box where he had them stored.

Before turning his attention back to the task at hand, Jack glanced around for his son. He figured the boy would be near his sister, but Alan was nowhere to be seen.

"Have you seen my son?" Jack called to the women.

"Not since you lifted him down from the wagon," Virginia responded.

With deep concern, Jack cupped his hands around his mouth and called, "Alan! Alan!"

No response.

A sense of panic welled in Jack's chest. If Alan had wandered away from camp, he could become lost or get hurt.

"If ya want to go look for your boy, I'll take care of the wheel," Cole offered.

Jack gave a nod. "Think I'd better check in all the wagons first. If Alan's not there, then I'll be heading into the woods to look for him."

Chapter 4

Jack called Alan's name again and again.

Still no response.

Jack looked in the back of his own wagon first, but there was no sign of Alan. Next he checked Cole's wagon. The boy wasn't there either. Just one more wagon to look in, and Jack would have no choice but to head for the woods.

Please let me find him, Lord, Jack prayed as he

hurried to Walter's wagon.

"Is there a problem?" Walter asked when Jack approached.

"I'm lookin' for my boy. Thought maybe he might have wandered over here and climbed inside your wagon."

Walter's forehead creased. "He'd better not be in there, or I'll tan the little runt's hide."

Jack's eyes narrowed as he glared at Walter. "Let's get one thing clear, Mr. Prentice. You are never to lay a hand on my son. Is that understood?"

"Then keep him away from my wagon!"

"I don't even know if he's here." Jack pulled the flap of the wagon open and blinked when he saw Alan crouched in one corner, holding a jar of candy. "What do you think you're doing?" he shouted, feeling anger and relief as he fought for control.

Alan hung his head and moved toward the open flap. "I wanted candy, Papa."

Before Jack could respond, Walter reached inside and snatched the jar from Alan. "Why, you little thief!" Red-faced, he turned to Jack. "What are you going to do about this?"

Jack lifted his son into his arms and set him on the ground. "It was wrong to get into Mr. Prentice's wagon and take his jar of candy. Now tell the man you're sorry and that you'll never do anything like that again."

"I–I'm sorry, mister." Alan's chin quivered.

Walter folded his arms and glared at the boy. "Well, you should be. If I was your father, I'd teach you a good lesson and you'd never steal from anyone again."

"He didn't exactly steal the jar of candy," Jack defended.

"He would have, if we hadn't caught him

in the act." Walter held the jar of candy close to his chest. "If anything like this ever happens again—"

"It won't. And don't worry. I'll make sure my boy stays clear of your wagon and your precious jar of candy." Hoisting Alan onto his shoulders, Jack headed back to his own wagon where he found Cole had finished putting the wheel back on.

"Glad to see you found your boy." Cole motioned to the wheel. "It's fixed, and we're set to roll. I saw you brought some grease along too, so I oiled it up for you."

"Thanks. Guess I should do that more often," Jack said. "I'll be ready in a minute. Just need to have a little talk with Alan."

As Cole headed for his horse, Jack set Alan on the wagon bench and took a seat beside him. "Now listen to me, son, and listen good.

What you did was wrong, and you need to be punished."

Tears welled in Alan's eyes. "Are ya gonna whip me, Papa?"

"No," Jack said, shaking his head. "But if the women fix dessert this evening, you won't be getting any. And you'll be goin' to bed as soon as we're done eating."

"Ya mean before Amelia?"

"Yes, your sister will get to stay up longer than you tonight."

"I'll be scared in that ole' wagon by myself," Alan whined.

"I'm sorry about that, but maybe some time alone in the dark will give you a chance to think about what you did today."

"Said I was sorry."

"Sorry is good, but God's Word tells us that it's wrong to steal, and I want you to realize that

and make sure it never happens again."

"It won't, Papa."

Jack raised his eyebrows and patted Alan's knee. "I'm glad to hear it. Now sit real still while I get your sister because it's time to get the wagons moving again."

As they continued their trek along the rutted trail, Cynthia sensed irritation in Walter. She'd never met a man as moody as him. His eyebrows always seemed to be furrowed, and for the last hour, he hadn't said more than a few words to her or Mama. Did she dare ask what was wrong, or would it be best to say nothing and hope he became more agreeable as the day wore on?

Deciding on the latter, Cynthia turned to Mama and said, "The next time we stop for a break, I'm going to get down from the wagon and walk. Sitting on this unyielding bench is

hard on my back, and it'll feel good to stretch my legs."

"Walking's not easy either," Mama complained. "It won't be long and the soles of our boots will have holes in them."

"It's a good thing we had the presence of mind to bring along more than one pair of boots," Cynthia said.

"Yes," Mama agreed, "but unless we walk less and ride more, two pair may not last till we get to California."

"You women are worried about nothing," Walter chimed in. "When we were back in Independence, I bought you both an extra pair of boots as well as a few new dresses. They're in the trunk with the other clothes."

Cynthia smiled, appreciative that he'd been so considerate. Perhaps Walter had more good qualities than she realized. He really did seem

to care about their welfare. Mama must have thought so too for she looked at Walter and smiled.

"Did ya get it?" Cole yelled in the direction of the gunfire. When they'd stopped for the night, Cole had left Walter with the women and children while he and Jack went hunting for fresh game.

"Yep. The feathers are still flying, but I got that big bird!" Jack hollered back.

"Wow!" Cole let out a whoop as he approached Jack on the other side of a small ridge. "That's a nice one."

"You bet." Jack grinned, obviously proud of the wild turkey he'd shot. "Everyone's bellies will be full tonight. I can taste this bird already."

Cole gave Jack a slap on the back. "Just look at the size of him. Why, I'll bet that turkey weighs at least twenty pounds."

"He's a big one—that's for sure."

"Guess we'd better get back to the wagons so we can get it cleaned and roasting over the campfire," Cole suggested after he'd offered to carry Jack's gun. "I'll let you carry your prize."

"Can't wait to see the look on everyone's face when we walk into camp with this," Jack said.

Jack was about to pick up the bird when Cole heard a low growl. He stopped abruptly. Jack did the same. The men looked at each other, but neither moved any farther.

"Here, take your gun." Cole handed Jack the gun he'd shot the turkey with. "Now, we're gonna turn around real slow."

They both turned in unison to face the growling menace. Standing on a rock a few feet away was a large gray wolf with its head lowered and teeth bared. Off to the right, stood another

one, and to the left a third wolf.

"Looks as if they want our supper," Jack whispered as the other two wolves started growling.

"They haven't come any closer. Maybe they're testing us," Cole said, hoping he was right. One thing was sure, he figured they were hungry and waiting to steal Jack's catch. Cole wasn't about to let that happen. "I hate to waste ammunition on those varmints, so let's make a lot of noise and see if that spooks 'em off."

"Sounds good to me," Jack agreed, so he and Cole started yelling and waving their arms.

Without breaking eye contact, Cole leaned down, picked up a hefty rock, and threw it at the biggest wolf. It must have been enough, because all three wolves ran into the woods.

"Come on, let's get outta here and head back to camp," Cole said as Jack picked up the turkey and slung it over his shoulder.

Jack led the way while Cole practically walked backward, making sure the wolves didn't return and chase after them. "We're gonna have to keep a watch for those wolves," he panted. "We only saw three, and hopefully, there's no more of 'em."

That evening, as they sat around the campfire, everyone seemed content after eating the meal they'd recently finished. Cynthia had to admit, eating turkey basted over an open fire was just as good, if not better, than the oven-roasted turkeys they'd had back home. It wasn't like the lavish meals they used to have, but cooked potatoes along with the succulent, tender turkey meat sure tasted good.

When Virginia brought out a pan of bread and some jam for dessert, Jack looked over at his boy and said, "None for you, son. Remember

what I said today?"

Alan hung his head.

"And it's time for you to go to bed."

"Amelia too?" Alan questioned.

"No, she gets to stay up for a while, remember?" Jack picked up his son and headed toward their wagon. While he put Alan to bed, Cynthia moved over to sit beside Amelia. She was such a pretty child and so well behaved. What a shame Amelia wouldn't talk. Cynthia was sure there was a lot to say locked inside the little girl. If there was just some way to get her to open up. Amelia did flash Virginia a small grin when she handed her some bread slathered with jam. Cynthia thought that was progress.

A short time later, Jack returned, and Virginia handed him a slice of bread with jelly.

"Thanks," he said, offering her a weary smile. It was clearly hard for him to make this trip

with two small children and no wife. Cynthia admired his determination to make a better life for Alan and Amelia in California. She hoped he did well as a cattle rancher.

Hearing a noise, Cynthia glanced to her left and was surprised to see Alan running away from Walter's wagon. Walter must have seen him at that moment as well, for he leapt up from the log where he sat and hollered, "Were you in my wagon again?"

With eyes wide and head hung low, Alan made a beeline for his father's wagon.

Cynthia held her breath, waiting to see what Jack would do, but before he made a move, the boy began to choke.

Cole, sitting the closest to Alan, jumped up, grabbed the child, and turned him upside-down. Then he gave Alan's back a good whack, and out popped a lemon drop. Everyone gasped, and

Alan started to howl. Whether it was from the trauma of choking or from fear of being found out, Cynthia didn't know.

Walter's face turned red, and he scowled at Jack. "I can't believe that boy stole from me again! I thought you had talked to him about this."

"Walter, it was only a piece of candy," Cynthia put in, hoping to diffuse his temper.

"No one asked you," he said sharply. "As I said earlier, that child needs to be taught a good lesson!"

"I did punish him," Jack said defensively. "And he will be punished again."

"Maybe you should remove the temptation," Virginia interjected, looking at Walter.

He frowned. "What's that supposed to mean?"

"Perhaps you should throw out the candy," she said. "Lemon drops can be dangerous,

especially for a child."

"Which is exactly why the little thief shouldn't be eating my candy!" Walter faced Jack with an angry expression. "You'd better take care of that boy of yours, because I'm not getting rid of my jar of candy!" With that, Walter stalked off toward his wagon like a stuck-up little rich boy instead of a grown man.

Cynthia cringed. She couldn't believe how stubborn and selfish Walter was being. Alan was only a child, and the temptation of Walter's candy was hard to pass up. Surely those lemon drops couldn't be that important to the man. Why couldn't he be kinder and have more patience like Jack?

"Well," Cole said, "I think it's best if we all head for bed. Mornin' comes quick, and since we're already behind in our travels, we need to get an early start tomorrow. So make sure you're

up bright and early."

Everyone headed to their wagons, and when Cynthia and her mother crawled into the back of Walter's wagon, Cynthia expressed her thoughts about Walter. Unfortunately, Mama didn't agree.

"Personally, I think Walter was right," Mama said. "I also believe that as his betrothed, you should support him on this matter, not take sides with a man like Jack."

"A man like Jack? What's that supposed to mean?" Cynthia questioned.

"He's clearly not a good father. What those children need is a mother to keep them in line."

Like you've always kept me in line? Cynthia thought. Ever since she was a child, she'd done whatever Mama said. *I wish I felt free to break my engagement to Walter and find something new and adventuresome to do. I fear that my life as Mrs. Walter Prentice will not be easy.*

Chapter 5

Dear Diary,

Cole says we're over halfway to California now, and even though we're all quite weary, everyone shares a sense of excitement.

We've had some setbacks along the way—repairs to the wagons, rain and mud bogging us down, and trouble crossing some

of the rivers, but nothing we weren't able to handle. Things are going along fairly well now, albeit slow, as some days we only make five miles or so. Other days we're able to travel ten to fifteen miles. We have given up catching the larger wagon train that went before us, but Cole thinks we're managing fine on our own. I pray he's right about that.

We must be on the right trail at least. We've passed several places along the way where things had been discarded, probably to lighten their load. Some of the pieces of furniture we saw had no doubt been beautiful once. I can't imagine how the people felt leaving behind belongings— perhaps family heirlooms—to rot away in this untamed wilderness.

Even sadder than seeing personal items

cast along the trail was looking at the occasional mounds of dirt with a wooden cross that had someone's name carved on it. I can't help wondering what took those people's lives. Was it smallpox, cholera, or some other disease? Or perhaps their deaths had been caused by something else. Thankfully, no one from our three wagons has gotten sick, so that's something to be grateful for.

Some time ago, I volunteered to take turns with Cole's sister to look after Jack's children during the day. They ride in Cole's wagon with Virginia during the morning hours and with me in their father's wagon throughout the afternoon. That has kept mischievous Alan out of trouble, and there's been no more of him sneaking into Walter's wagon in search of candy. The boy really

isn't a bad child. He's just curious and eager like most boys his age. Alan's sister, Amelia, still hasn't spoken, but she's an agreeable child and does whatever she's told. In the evenings when we've stopped for the night, the children hover close to their father, especially when those terrible wolves start to howl. I don't think I'll ever get used to that eerie noise. It frightened me when Cole told how he and Jack had encountered some wolves, and I've been wary ever since. I try not to think about it, but sometimes it sounds as if the wolves are right outside our camp, and I'm afraid they might be following us.

Virginia and I are well acquainted by now, and I find her to be quite pleasant. She talks a lot about Cole's dream of finding gold and also how eager she is to teach

school once they're settled in California.
I wish I could say that I was as eager to
get there as Virginia is, but maybe I'll feel
differently once we arrive.

Cynthia sighed and lifted her pen as her thoughts turned back to Alan and Amelia. Spending time with Jack's children made her wish she was a mother. Maybe she would be someday, but it still concerned her as to what kind of father Walter would make. No matter how hard she tried to fight it, Cynthia was nowhere near ready to become Walter's wife. He could be so stuffy at times when she herself was so full of life. Sometimes it felt as if she were bursting at the seams.

But what other choice do I have? she thought, glancing at Walter as he took his seat on the bench and gathered up the reins. *I accepted his*

proposal and gave Mama my word that I'd marry him, so I can't back out of it now. Besides, Mama and I would have no way to support ourselves once we get to California, so I need to get the crazy notion out of my head that there is someone better for me than Walter.

Mable watched her daughter out of the corner of her eye, wondering what she was thinking. She hoped it wasn't about Jack or Cole.

These days Cynthia said very little to Walter, and that concerned Mable. What worried her even more was how attached Cynthia had become to Jack's children, acting as if she were their mother. As she rode in Jack's wagon with Alan and Amelia, no doubt making conversation with their father, Mable had seen the way Jack looked at Cynthia—like she was something special. Cole looked at her that way as well and often made snide remarks about Walter

whenever Cynthia was around. Was he trying to poison her against the man she was engaged to marry? Did Cole think he was better than Walter because he had more knowledge about wilderness survival and could do many things with his hands? Walter could do things too—things neither Cole nor Jack were capable of. Walter was a smart man when it came to business dealings, and in Mable's book, that meant a lot.

I need to keep an eye on things, she told herself, swatting at a pesky fly buzzing around her head. *My top priority is making sure Cynthia doesn't get any ideas about Jack or Cole and goes through with the wedding once we get to California. After all, Walter's a much better catch for my daughter than either of those men. He's a lot wealthier too.*

"When we gonna get to Californy?" Alan asked, tugging on the sleeve of Virginia's dress.

"It's California," she patiently replied. "And we'll get there when we get there."

"Papa says 'fore Christmas."

Virginia nodded. "I'm sure we'll be there in plenty of time for Christmas."

"Does Santy Claus know the way to Californy?" the boy questioned.

She let go of the reins with one hand and gave the boy's knee a quick pat. "I'm sure he will be able to find it."

"That's good, 'cause I wouldn't wanna live there if Santa couldn't come."

Virginia smiled, remembering how when she and Cole were children, they used to sneak downstairs on Christmas Eve after everyone was in bed planning to wait up for Santa. They'd never gotten a glimpse of him and had always fallen asleep. She could see little Alan doing something like that. With his determined spirit,

he'd probably stay awake all night in the hopes of getting a look at Santa Claus as he put presents under the tree.

"What about you, Amelia?" Virginia asked. "Are you looking forward to spending Christmas in your new home?"

The girl gave no reply, not even a nod or shake of her head. Instead, she stared at her hands, clasped tightly in her lap.

I wish I knew what she was thinking, Virginia thought. *If only I could think of something to say or do that would pull the sweet little girl out of her world of silence.*

Being a schoolteacher, Virginia had dealt with children who had all sorts of problems, but none were locked in a world of silence like Amelia. She wondered if the child would always be like this or if there was a possibility of her speaking again.

As Cole urged his horse forward, ever mindful of what was ahead, he couldn't help but worry. Days on the trail had turned into weeks, and weeks into months. They'd gone over South Pass, and their last stop for supplies and fresh animals to pull the wagons had been at Fort Hall. Now they were following the Humboldt River in the direction of the Sierra Nevada.

They were behind where they should be by this time, but from what they'd seen left from previous wagon trains, they must be on the right trail. But Cole had other matters to be uneasy about. He was anxious not only about another incident with wolves or some other wild animal, but about the possibility of encountering bad weather—particularly snow—before they reached California. Warm

days were being replaced with chilly mornings, and at some point they were bound to hit snow. He hoped it wouldn't amount to much and that they could make it to their destination before any bad weather set in. It wouldn't be good for them to get trapped in the mountains due to foul weather. He hadn't shared his concerns with the others, not even Ginny. For now, it was best to keep those thoughts to himself.

Thanks to the wind that had recently whipped up, they were moving slowly again—too slow to suit Cole. The trees seemed to groan as they swayed from the force of the wind, and a light drizzle had begun to fall. Even the oxen seemed miserable, plodding along at a slower pace.

So far, they hadn't run out of food. Between the supplies that were packed in their three wagons and the game that had been available

whenever he and Jack hunted, none of them went to bed hungry. Cole had to admit he couldn't wait for a good home-cooked meal that Ginny would make once they got settled in California. For now, rabbits and the occasional sage hen would have to do, along with the never-ending beans that seemed to accompany most evening meals.

He glanced behind at the wagons and tipped his hat when Ginny waved at him. She had Jack's children riding with her, and the smile on her face said it all. His sister had a fondness for children, and it showed. She was a good schoolteacher, and he was equally sure she'd be a good mother someday. Unfortunately, his sister had never had a steady beau other than that creep Clay Summers. After Clay jilted Ginny, she never got interested in anyone else. Maybe it was because she'd been

too busy teaching, but more than likely it had to do with her shyness around men. From what Cole had been told, California was home to a lot of men, so if Ginny came out of her shell, she was bound to find a husband. She certainly enjoyed fussing over Jack's kids. Each morning she fixed Amelia's hair and made sure both children washed up. Cole felt sorry for Jack. It couldn't be easy losing a wife and trying to raise two youngsters by himself.

Cole wanted to get married someday and settle down. But first he needed to find gold. He knew it was a risky way to make money, but he had to give it a chance. Yet in the back of his mind was one nagging thought: *What if I spend all my money on supplies, only to come up empty-handed and never get rich?*

Chapter 6

Dear Diary,

We've come to the foot of the Sierra Nevadas and started up the Truckee River. Unfortunately, things haven't gone well. One of our oxen has died, and to make things worse, yesterday it began to snow. It's very rocky here, and since we've had to work our way around the rocks, we've only made it a

short distance in two days.

This morning it's still snowing, and I'm worried. What will we do if it gets worse?

I must close now, as Cole just rode up to our wagon and said it was time to move out. I didn't like the concern I saw on his face, and when I asked if he thought we were going to be okay, he just gave a quick nod and rode away. His silence spoke volumes.

"I don't like this. I don't like it one bit," Walter complained as he got their wagon moving. "If this weather gets any worse, we could be stuck out here in the wilderness with no protection from the elements except our wagons. My hands are frozen, and my gloves aren't helping anymore."

Mama's face blanched. "Oh dear, haven't we

been through enough already? Do you really think we might get stranded in the snow?"

Walter shrugged, blowing into his gloves for more warmth. "Guess it all depends on how bad it gets."

Cynthia reached over and gently patted Mama's arm. Even though she felt concern about the snow, she didn't want her mother to worry. "Try not to fret. I'm sure we'll be fine. We need to pray and ask God to take care of us."

Mama nodded slowly, but Walter just grunted.

After all, Cynthia reasoned, *it does no good to dwell on something that's out of our control.* She watched as Walter pulled his hat down tighter on his head. *Poor Walter. I don't think he could be any more miserable. This kind of existence is definitely not for a man like him. Of course, it's not exactly my cup of tea either. I'd rather be home in*

New York than here on the trail, bouncing around on a hard seat in terrible weather. Somehow, the adventure of going to California has worn off.

Cynthia thought about Cole's wagon ahead of them and wondered how Jack's children were doing as they sat up front with Virginia. Amelia and Alan would be riding with Virginia all day, since Jack needed to stay in his own wagon. Cynthia wanted to ride in Jack's wagon with the children but figured with the way Walter had been acting lately, he'd probably have something negative to say about it. He'd become quite protective of her lately, acting as if they were already married. Just the other day when Jack was talking to her about the children, Walter stepped up to him and said, "I hope you don't get used to Cynthia taking care of your children, because as soon as we reach Sutter's Fort, we'll be going our separate ways."

How embarrassing, Cynthia thought, pulling the brim of her bonnet down in an effort to shield her face from the blinding snow. *I'm sure Jack realizes I won't always be there to help with Amelia and Alan. I should have spoken up when Walter told Jack that, instead of turning away with regret. Is it always going to be this way—Walter treating me like a piece of property and acting like he owns me?*

Another time when Cole was talking to them, Walter had told Cole in no uncertain terms to stop gawking at Cynthia. Cole had looked at Walter like he was mad, and Cynthia had fumed at the mere suggestion, although she'd said nothing to Walter. Obviously he disliked Cole, and she didn't want to say or do anything to make it worse. Cole had every right to respond negatively toward Walter, but Cynthia admired how he had simply turned and walked away.

When the wagons stopped for the night, Cole waited until Jack's children were in bed then gathered the adults together. "With the way the snow's been comin' down all day," he said, "I'm afraid we may have to hunker down somewhere for a few days and give our oxen time to rest."

"Are you crazy? And just where might that 'somewhere' be?" Walter shouted, spreading his arms out and looking around. "If we sit here with our wagons, we're likely to freeze to death. Besides, we've little protection from the elements, so I say we keep moving."

"If we had a better place to get out of the weather, it would be good if we stopped traveling for a few days," Jack put in.

The women all nodded in agreement.

"Well, we don't have a better place," Cole said. "So we have two choices. We can either stay

put with our wagons for a day or two, or we can keep moving and hope the oxen don't give out. With the snow bogging us down, it's putting an extra strain on what little strength those poor animals have left. If we don't stay put, we'll have to start lessening the loads in our wagons to make it easier for the oxen. We've already lost one, and I don't want to lose more."

Cole watched as Cynthia's mother bit her lip, no doubt thinking about his words.

"Let's take a vote," Walter said. "How many are in favor of us moving up the trail come morning?"

Jack, Mable, Cynthia, and Walter raised their hands. "That's a majority, so it's settled. We head out in the morning."

"Wait a minute, now," Cole said, glaring at Walter. "I thought I was the one in charge here."

"You were supposed to be leading us up the

trail," Walter reminded, "but that doesn't mean we have to agree with or do everything you say."

Cole grimaced. It seemed to him that the irritating man hadn't agreed with anything he'd done so far, but against his better judgment, he'd go along with everyone's wishes and leave in the morning. It didn't mean it was a good idea though. All he could do was try to get a decent night's sleep and see how things shaped up in the morning. Maybe they'd get lucky and it would quit snowing.

By the next evening, the snow that had begun falling earlier had turned into a blizzard. The blinding snow came down sideways, making it hard to see anything at all. There was no doubt about it: they were definitely lost. If that wasn't bad enough, Cole had no idea what to do for the people in his charge. Unless

the weather improved, they'd be trapped here in the Sierra Nevadas. If only they could find some better shelter. Their covered wagons didn't offer enough protection from a storm such as this. Even if they survived the storm, what was going to happen when they ran out of food? Would they end up like the Donner party who had gotten trapped at Truckee Lake a few years ago? Many had died during the tragic ordeal, and worse, some of the dead had become food for those who still lived.

Cole gulped and looked heavenward. *Dear Lord, please don't let a terrible thing like that happen to us. Give me the wisdom to know what to do, or provide us with a miracle so no one will perish.*

Chapter 7

Dear Diary,

*We're in the worst possible situation.
Not only are we in the middle of a terrible
snowstorm, but Cole says we're stranded
and he can't find the trail. Once again,
Cole has left Walter and Jack here with the
women and children while he goes hunting
for fresh meat.*

Are we stuck here until spring? Could we even survive that long? Have we come this far only to have it end in tragedy? I'm really getting concerned. It's so cold and hard to function. I'm colder than I've ever been before. My teeth chatter so hard I'm afraid they might break. All any of us can do at this point is pray that God will spare us.

Tears splashed on the paper, smearing the last few words of Cynthia's journal entry. She sniffed and wiped her nose. "Oh Mama, I'm so scared. I wish we'd stayed in New York instead of letting Walter talk us into making this trek through the wilderness, which can only end in our demise."

"Don't let Walter hear you talking like that," Mama warned, glancing toward the lean-to

Walter was trying to set up with Jack's help. "He thought he was doing the right thing, and it's not his fault the weather's turned bad or that we've had so many delays. If things had gone as they should, we'd be in California by now." Mama's lips pursed. "I blame Cole for that too."

"It's not his fault we ran into snow," Cynthia said in Cole's defense. Briskly, she rubbed her arms, hoping to stimulate warmth in her limbs.

"That's true," Mama agreed, "but he should have kept the wagons moving faster."

"Mama, he did the best he could, and he's not to blame for any of the setbacks we've had."

Mama sighed. "I can't believe he left us here in the middle of this storm to go hunting. He's likely to get lost out there in the snow. Then what'll we do?"

"We need fresh meat," Cynthia said, although she was equally anxious. What if Cole got lost in

the woods and they never saw him again? "Don't worry, Mama. He'll be back soon." Cynthia's gaze went to where she'd last seen Cole walking in the deep snow with his gun, hoping against hope for his safe return.

Cole yanked the brim of his hat down, as he trudged through the forest on makeshift snowshoes, looking for wild game. So far he'd seen nothing, not even a rabbit. *Guess the animals are bedded down or burrowed in till after the storm,* he thought. With the snow swirling around him, he didn't dare venture too far, because the last thing he needed was to get lost and be unable to find his way back to camp.

Moving a little farther, he was taken by surprise when he spotted a small cabin. No smoke rose from the chimney, and he couldn't see any livestock or other sign of life outside the cabin.

Cautiously, Cole approached and knocked on the door.

No response. The only sounds to be heard were the wind blowing through the pines and the snow filtering down as it blew off the branches.

Opening the door and peering guardedly inside, Cole called, "Anybody here?"

No response.

He waited a few minutes then lit a match. Seeing a lantern on a small wooden table, he lit that, and instantly the cabin became illuminated. After a quick scan of the two small rooms, Cole knew with certainty that the cabin had been abandoned.

Cole pulled his coat collar tighter around his neck. It was cold inside the cabin, and while there didn't appear to be any food on the shelves, this would be a place for them to get in out of the weather and hunker down

until spring if necessary. There was a fireplace, and a small stack of firewood outside the cabin would get them started until they found more. The biggest problem would be keeping them in food. Cole thought between the supplies they still had, plus any game he or Jack might bag, they could survive. At least he hoped that would be the case.

Closing the cabin door behind him, Cole started back for the wagons, thankful for the tracks his snowshoes had left in the snow. He figured everyone would be glad with the news he was about to bring them. Staying in this cabin would be better than trying to survive in their wagons, which he doubted they'd be able to do much longer.

"I found an abandoned cabin in the woods where we can take refuge," Cole announced when he entered the camp and found everyone gathered under the lean-to Jack and Walter had constructed. He bent over, trying to catch his breath after trudging back through the heavy snow. Sweat that had been worked up during the vigorous return was replaced with chills seeping right through his skin.

"What about our wagons? Can we get them and the livestock through the woods?" Jack questioned.

"I think so," Cole answered, rubbing his hands as he held them over the fire. "It might take us awhile in this snow, but we need to try."

"Is there food in the cabin or any other supplies?" Walter asked.

Cole shook his head. "No food, but there's a fireplace, a table, and a few chairs. I think with what we have in our wagons, if we ration the food we should be okay."

"What about fresh meat?" This question

came from Cynthia's mother. "Were you able to shoot anything while you were in the woods?"

"I didn't see any game, but after I found the cabin, I quit lookin'." Cole motioned to the wagons. "Right now I think we need to head for that cabin. Once we get there, we can discuss sleeping arrangements and how we're gonna survive till the weather improves."

Walter sneered at Cole. "Don't you mean, *if* it improves? We could be stuck here until spring—if we live that long."

Alan started to cry, and he looked up at his dad. "Are we gonna die, Papa?"

"No, son," Jack assured the boy, before giving Walter an icy stare. "Not if I can help it."

Amelia's chin quivered, but she said nothing. It was obvious that both of Jack's children were afraid.

Feeling the need to calm everyone's fears,

Cole said, "I think we can find plenty of fresh game. We'll have a sturdy roof over our heads and be warmer. There's a fireplace for warmth and to melt snow for water. We have plenty of beans left, so if nothing else, we can survive on bean soup."

Walter wrinkled his nose. "Oh good, I can hardly wait for that."

"What about Christmas, Cole?" Virginia spoke up. "I'd hoped we'd be in California to celebrate the holiday."

"We'll just have to wait and see how it goes," Cole replied. No way would he make them any promises.

Surprisingly, Walter was the first to start for his wagon. Everyone else did the same, and Cole mounted his horse. They'd soon be headed to the safety of the cabin, and maybe come morning things would look better.

Cynthia was anxious to go, but before getting into Walter's wagon, she paused to thank the Lord for leading Cole to the cabin and for keeping him safe. She was about to add more to her words of thanks when Walter, helping her into the wagon, said, "Well, isn't that just wonderful? Who knows how long we'll have to stay cooped up with everyone in that cabin before we can head out again."

Cynthia sighed with exasperation. "You should be glad God has gotten us this far and that He led Cole to the cabin. What's more, we ought to be thankful nothing happened to Cole while he was out there looking for fresh game."

"Oh, is that how you see it?" Walter shot back. "Well maybe you should ask yourself why, if Cole is so perfect as you seem to believe, aren't

we in California by now like we are supposed to be?"

"Nobody can predict the unknown, Walter." With her arms crossed, Cynthia held her ground. "I think Cole's done a great job so far. Which is more than I can say for you," she quickly added, surprised at her ability to speak up to Walter like this. Maybe Mama's outspokenness was beginning to rub off on her.

Walter's face flamed as his eyes narrowed into tiny slits. "What exactly is that supposed to mean?"

"You haven't gone hunting, not even once, and you don't—"

"Now hold on a minute, missy. I may not be good at firing a gun or gutting a deer, but I have managed to drive the oxen pulling our wagon, and that ought to count for something." Walter's finger shook as he pointed at Cynthia. "And

don't forget that you have agreed to become my wife, so your loyalty should be to me, not some fellow who thinks he knows everything."

"This isn't about loyalty," she argued. "I just think you should realize that Cole has done his best by us and try to be more grateful."

Walter's face hardened, and his gaze bored into her. Just as quickly, his expression softened. "My dear, we are all quite tired. So let's stop quarreling and go see what this cabin is like. I suppose it'll be better than me sleeping in a tent, or you and Mable taking refuge in the cold wagon."

Cynthia relaxed some, and when the wagons headed out, she was almost glad for all the obstacles that had slowed their travels these last couple of months. Maybe there was a reason for the delays, giving her time to rethink things. Right now, she wasn't sure she was ready to

become Mrs. Walter Prentice. But did she have the nerve to tell him that? If she could choose another man, who would it be?

Chapter 8

Dear Diary,

    *I can't believe we've been cooped up
in this cabin together for eight long weeks
with no letup in the weather. If anything,
the snow and frigid temperatures have
gotten worse. There's so much snow piled on
the cabin's roof, I'm afraid it might cave in.*

    Wild animals are scarce, and fishing is

almost impossible due to the frozen river. We're running dangerously low on food, and if the men aren't able to find fresh game soon, they'll be forced to slaughter our oxen. It's hard to find wood for the fire as well, and everyone is sick of eating beans.

Tempers are flaring and sharp words have been exchanged, especially between Walter and Cole. Last night Walter accused Cole of trying to kiss me, which is ridiculous, since we are never alone. I think the stress of what we are going through has caused Walter to have irrational thoughts. I have to admit though, Cole looks at me strangely sometimes. Is it a look of desire I see on his handsome face, or does he feel sorry for me, being engaged to a man like Walter?

Jack's children grow restless, and little

Alan whines much of the time, which I'm sure gets on everyone's nerves. Virginia and I take turns trying to occupy the children, but there's only so much we can do with them.

Remembering the words of Colossians 4:2, I pray every day that God will bring us out of this travesty, even though, at this point, it seems futile. Short of a miracle, we could very well die in this tiny cabin.

"I hate being cooped up like this," Cynthia's mother complained. She wrapped her shawl tightly around her shoulders and moved closer to the fireplace, where Cynthia, Virginia, and the children were huddled.

"I know it's hard, Mama," Cynthia said, setting her journal aside. "At least we have a place to keep dry and somewhat warm, and it's

a lot better than the protection we would get from trying to live in our covered wagons."

"You're right about that," Virginia agreed. "I'm thankful my brother found this abandoned cabin when he did, or we'd have frozen to death by now."

Cynthia looked around their simple dwelling. Since arriving, the womenfolk had cleaned the cabin the best they could, using a broom Virginia had in her and Cole's wagon. Each of the women had brought in a few other things as well to give the cabin a homey feel. A red checkered cloth covered the table, and they'd used a piece of material from Mama's trunk to drape over the window. It wasn't the frilly curtains that had adorned the windows in their home back East, but it added some color to the once-drab room. Jack had used the wheel grease to plug a few drafty holes they'd found

in the cabin walls, and it was definitely warmer in the tiny abode than what they'd been used to in their drafty wagons.

"We'll be out of wood soon, and then what will we do for heat?" Mama asked, frowning. "Nothing we experienced on the trail before the blizzard hit was as bad as this—not the broken wagon parts, seeing those Indians, ferocious thunderstorms, deep rivers to cross, steep mountain trails, hordes of mosquitoes, or frightening wolves." Her voice trembled, and Cynthia knew her mother was close to tears. Cynthia felt that she must try to put on a brave front in order to offer courage and hope to her mother. The trouble was, she didn't feel courageous or hopeful at the moment. In fact, she'd never been more scared or discouraged. If worse came to worst, would they have to start using things they'd brought along to burn

in place of real firewood? And when they ran out of food, how long would it be before they starved to death?

Of course Jack, in his gentle, positive way, kept telling his children that everything would be okay. When little Alan mentioned Christmas and asked if Santa Claus would find them, Jack had patted his son's head and said he was sure Santa would come and that they'd have a Christmas no matter what.

But what kind of Christmas can we have here, with no tree to decorate, no gifts to give, and so little food to go around? Cynthia asked herself. *There is certainly nothing festive or tasty about bean soup or chewy venison jerky. I hope Cole and Jack have success wherever they are hunting right now.* She glanced toward the back room, where Walter had gone to rest on a cot. He'd complained of a headache earlier and said he needed to lie down.

Mama had gone in to check on him awhile ago and returned to the main room, saying he'd fallen asleep.

I wonder if he faked a headache to avoid going outside in the cold and helping Jack and Cole look for a deer or some other wild game. He certainly doesn't carry his weight around here like the other men do. The only thing Walter's really good at is complaining and telling others what he thinks they should do. I'm beginning to believe he must have been quite spoiled when he was growing up, used to getting his own way and pouting when he didn't.

"Let's try to make the best of things, Mable, and trust the Lord to see us through," Virginia said, smiling and pushing Cynthia's thoughts aside. Cynthia could see though that Virginia's smile was forced. Truth be told, she was probably frightened, but for the children's sake, sweet

Virginia was trying not to let on.

"Let's read some verses of scripture," Virginia suggested. "Hearing God's Word always makes me feel better."

"That's a good idea," Cynthia agreed. "It'll help pass the time while Jack and Cole are out hunting."

Virginia went to get the Bible from her reticule, and the women took seats at the table while the children reclined on a blanket near the fire. Opening the Bible, Virginia said, "Here's a verse from 1 Peter 5 that offers hope when we feel depressed: 'Casting all your care upon him; for he careth for you.' " She turned to another passage. "Psalm 31:24 says, 'Be of good courage, and he shall strengthen your heart, all ye that hope in the Lord.' "

Mama sighed and clasped her hands. "It's hard to be strong and wait for the Lord when

we're not sure if He will rescue us from this seemingly hopeless situation."

"That's why we must continue to pray and trust Him to answer our petitions," Virginia said.

"I believe what you're saying is true," Cynthia interjected, "but my faith has weakened. Things really do look hopeless," she whispered, in case Alan and Amelia were still awake.

"When our hope is lost, that's when we need to rely fully on Him, for with God, all things are possible." Virginia clasped the other women's hands. "Shall we pray?"

Both women nodded.

"Heavenly Father," Virginia quietly prayed. "Calm our fears and give us hope. Help us to trust You, even when things seem hopeless. Protect the men as they search for food, and we ask You to provide for all of our needs. Amen."

When Cynthia opened her eyes, she saw

Amelia staring up at her with an angelic expression. It tugged on Cynthia's heart. She didn't know how, but she was determined to see that Jack's precious children had a merry Christmas.

"If we don't bag a deer or even a rabbit today, we'll need to come up with something else to feed our group," Cole said to Jack as they traipsed through the woods on the snowshoes they'd made.

"We're not quite out of beans yet," Jack reminded.

Cole rolled his eyes and groaned. "I've never cared for beans that much, but I can honestly say that if I never saw another bean again, it would be fine with me."

Jack smiled. "I agree. That's why we need to bag a deer."

"Let's hope that won't take too long, 'cause if we don't find food, we may not have long to live."

Jack's smile turned upside down. "I wish you wouldn't talk like that."

"Just statin' facts as I see 'em." Cole stopped walking and looked up. The snow had stopped, but it was still extremely cold, and he seriously doubted that the snow already on the ground would melt before spring. "I've been wondering about something, Jack."

"What's that?"

"Do you think Cynthia's in love with Walter?"

Jack shrugged his shoulders. "I don't know, but they're planning to get married, so I guess she must love him."

Cole huffed, "I don't see how any woman could love a crotchety, arrogant man like that, much less a lady as sweet and pretty as Cynthia."

Jack's eyebrows lifted as he stared at Cole. "Are you interested in Cynthia? Is that why you're wondering if she's in love with Walter?"

Cole rubbed his chin as he thought about the best way to answer Jack's question. The truth was, if Cynthia wasn't engaged to be married, he'd have already made his intentions known. But it didn't seem right to move in on another man's territory, even if that man was an irritating fellow like "Mr. Fancy Pants."

"Cole, did ya hear what I said?" Jack asked, bumping Cole's arm.

"Yeah, I heard. Just wasn't sure how to answer." Cole paused and rubbed his chin. "Uh, you're not interested in Cynthia, are ya, Jack?"

"Well, um. . . You're right. She is pretty, and my kids like her too." Jack's gaze dropped to the snow-covered ground. "Truth is, I. . ."

Hearing a sudden noise, Cole turned in

time to see a nice-sized buck step out of the bushes a few yards away. Immediately, he took aim and fired. The buck dropped to the ground, and Cole breathed a sigh of relief. They wouldn't go hungry tonight at least. For that matter, the venison they'd get from this big fellow should last a good many days. Maybe, as Virginia often said, God was truly watching out for them. If that was the case, Cole hoped God's mercy would continue until the spring thaw.

Chapter 9

Dear Diary,

Tonight is Christmas Eve. Mama,
Virginia, and I have been busy all day
preparing for tomorrow, hoping to make it
special for Jack's children. The men brought
in a small pine tree with soft needles. We've
decorated it the best we can with pinecones,
paper snowflakes, and pieces of colorful

yarn we tied into bows on the tips of each bough.

Earlier in the week, Cole brought in some freshly broken pine branches that worked perfectly for making garland. We women were able to bind enough together to hang over the cabin's one window and doorway. Now, with both the tree and garland, it even smells like Christmas here in the cabin. Virginia cut out a star and Jack put it on top of the tree.

I went outside to get a few more pinecones this afternoon, and Walter followed. I thought at first he'd come to help, but then he pulled me into his arms and tried to kiss me. When I turned my face away and said I was saving my kisses until our wedding night, he said I was acting like an immature child and that he

had every right to kiss me. I was relieved when Jack walked past, interrupting us, but Walter looked none too happy about it. I quickly returned to the cabin to help Virginia and Mama wrap a few gifts for the children in pieces of cloth and place them under the tree. We each found some things in our wagons we thought Alan and Amelia might like. I'm giving Amelia the china-head doll Papa gave me when I was a child. I probably shouldn't have brought it along, but I just couldn't part with it. Now it seems more important to give it to Amelia than to hang on to it for sentimental reasons. For Alan, I have a set of dominoes. I think he'll have fun playing with them.

Virginia plans to give both children a small blackboard with eraser and chalk.

They should enjoy that as well. My prayer is that the children will have a special Christmas and we'll all make it safely to California in the spring.

Since our food supply has dwindled to almost nothing, there will be no fancy Christmas meal tomorrow. Instead, we'll each have a bowl of venison stew, for which I know I should feel appreciation, but I'd really hoped for a turkey. I guess I ought to be grateful that we haven't starved to death. Prayers and faith to believe that God is still with us are what's keeping me from giving in to despair.

Cynthia looked around at the dwelling that had been their home for a good many weeks. When they'd first settled in, they had plenty of arguments from being cooped up in

such cramped quarters, but after a while, the nitpicking stopped, and they realized what had to be done. Knowing their survival depended on it, the weary pioneers settled into a routine and worked together.

Cole and Jack searched for firewood and went hunting, occasionally coming back with small game. Thankfully, the little rabbits and squirrels provided meat and also helped to make their dwindling food supplies last a bit longer.

The women took turns bringing in buckets of snow to melt in the pot they used for cooking. Between them, they were able to prepare simple dishes, adding to what the hunters had been able to provide.

Walter was another story. He kept busy doing mediocre tasks, but mostly sat at the table, pen and tablet at hand, figuring out details concerning the businesses he planned to

open once they got to California, and checking his watch for the time. Sometimes he would surprise everyone and bring in some firewood while Jack and Cole were out hunting. But if the other men were there, Walter let them do most of the work. Cynthia was surprised there weren't more arguments, especially where Walter was concerned. But everyone seemed tolerant. What was the point in arguing with him when he was so set in his ways?

Cynthia couldn't help being a little excited though. She'd always loved the Christmas holiday, and with the special touches they'd managed inside the humble abode, it actually felt like Christmas. The little pine tree, with its few decorations, almost seemed prettier than the Christmas trees Cynthia remembered from the past. While there weren't any store-bought ornaments or fancy garland, this tree, in all its

simplicity, was like no other. It was amazing how a little tree could do so much to lift one's spirits, and in their precarious situation, it was certainly needed.

"Sure wish I could give my kids a better Christmas," Jack said as he and Cole began cutting up a tree that had recently fallen. Just as they'd been about to run out of the fallen deadwood they'd been able to gather in the area, a huge dead white fir tree not far from the cabin had toppled over, unable to bear the weight of the snow. It was a miracle from heaven that would provide them warmth for a while longer. Despite their situation, it seemed that God was intervening, giving hope each time they felt defeated.

"Kids are kids. I'm sure they'll be happy with the few gifts Virginia and Cynthia are planning to give 'em," Cole said.

"That may be, but I do have a gift for each of them," Jack responded. "I have a small wooden horse that I carved for Alan, and I'm givin' Amelia her mother's locket."

"I'll bet they'll like those things." Cole bent down and picked up an armload of wood. "Guess I'd better take this to the cabin. Then I think one or both of us oughta go hunting. We haven't had any fresh meat since I shot that deer a few weeks ago, and the women will be cooking what little we have left for our Christmas dinner."

"You're right," Jack agreed. "If we don't find some game soon, we'll once again be in jeopardy of starving."

"Didn't want to say anything in front of the kids, but I saw wolf tracks beyond those trees yesterday mornin'. We'll have to be careful when we go hunting and make sure we stay close

together from here on out."

"Good idea. I haven't forgotten what happened before. Why don't we go out on Christmas morning and see what we can find? It's a cinch that Walter won't make an effort to help us find any game. He sits around with the women all day, checkin' the time, counting his money, and making plans for those businesses he wants to open if we ever make it to California."

Jack grimaced. "You mean, *when* we get to California, don't ya?"

"Yeah, that's what I meant," Cole corrected. Truth was, at this point, he wasn't sure they'd ever make it out of these mountains.

That evening after everyone had eaten their venison stew, Cynthia suggested they sing some Christmas carols.

"That's a good idea," Virginia agreed. "But

before we sing, maybe one of the men would like to read the Christmas story from the Bible."

"I'd be glad to do that," Jack said, smiling at Virginia. "It wouldn't seem like Christmas without reading how God sent His Son to earth as a baby."

"Is Santa comin' tonight after we go to bed?" Alan asked, looking hopefully at his father.

Jack gave the boy's back a light thump. "There'll be a few Christmas presents for you and your sister in the morning; don't ya worry about that."

Apparently satisfied with his father's reply, Alan climbed onto Virginia's lap, while Amelia rested comfortably on Cynthia's lap, and they listened to Jack start the story.

Cynthia looked at her mother and wondered if she was remembering past Christmases. Oh, how she missed Papa reading them the same

story. She closed her eyes and could almost hear her father's deep voice repeating the words Jack now read.

After the story was over, they sang some favorite carols with Jack accompanying them on his mouth harp bringing merriment to the cabin. Cole sang the loudest, and Cynthia suppressed a giggle. No doubt, the songs held precious memories for him too. Even Walter joined in, but Cynthia wondered if it was because he wanted to outdo Cole. *Forgive me, Lord. I shouldn't think such thoughts. I'm glad if Walter's feeling the Christmas spirit.*

As they sang "O Come, All Ye Faithful," Cynthia felt a sense of peace. Tonight this quaint little cabin was full of good cheer, something each of them needed.

They'd just started the second stanza of "Joy to the World" when the cabin door flew open.

A gray-haired man with a matching beard, wearing a buffalo robe and carrying a pack over his shoulder, stepped into the cabin, bringing snowflakes and cold air with him. Blinking his eyes several times, he stared at them with a look of astonishment.

Before any of the adults could utter a word, Amelia pointed to the man and exclaimed, "Santa Claus!"

Chapter 10

Cynthia didn't know what had surprised her more: seeing the big, bearded man who'd entered the cabin unannounced or hearing Amelia speak. Probably the latter, she decided, for it wasn't just astonishing; it was downright miraculous—especially on this very special night.

"Oh Amelia, my sweet girl," Jack cried,

scooping his daughter into his arms. "It's so good to hear you talking again."

"Santa Claus came to see us, Papa," she said, smiling widely as she stared at the stranger who'd entered the cabin.

Was Amelia suddenly released from the emotional trap that had held her captive all this time? Cynthia wondered.

Eyes sparkling brightly, showing life from within, Jack's daughter giggled as any child would at seeing the whiskered Santa. The little girl couldn't take her eyes off the man and neither could Alan.

"I ain't Santa Claus, and I'd like to know what you all are doin' in my cabin," the man said gruffly, his gaze traveling from person to person. Then he quickly shut the door.

"We're a small wagon train heading to California," Cole spoke up. "When the weather

turned bad and we couldn't go any farther, we took refuge here, thinking the place was abandoned."

"Well, it ain't. My name's Abe Jones, and this here cabin you've taken over is mine." The man's tone softened as he looked at Amelia and Alan staring up at him with wide-eyed expressions. "Sorry to disappoint ya 'bout Santa Claus." He gave his beard a quick pull. "Guess I do kinda look like him."

"If this is your cabin, then why was there no sign of life when we got here several weeks ago, and where have you been all this time?" Walter questioned.

"I was visiting my wife's tribe, like I've done every year since Two Moons died ten years ago," Abe explained.

Walter's eyebrows lifted high on his forehead. "You were married to an Indian?"

Abe gave a nod. "You got somethin' to say about that?" His steely blue eyes narrowed as he glared at Walter, challenging him to say more.

Oh please, Walter, don't make any trouble, Cynthia thought. *If you offend this man further, he's likely to throw us out in the cold.*

"I'm sure Mr. Prentice didn't mean anything by his question," Cole was quick to say. "We're sorry for intruding, but we needed shelter. Guess we're just surprised to learn that someone owns this cabin."

"Yep," Abe said, tossing his pack on the floor and going to stand in front of the fireplace. "Built it with my own two hands after Two Moons and I were married." He paused and rubbed his hands briskly together. "As I said before, I've been holed up with Two Moon's Shoshone kin, so that's why the cabin looked empty."

"If you were living with your wife's family,

then why'd you come back here in the dead of winter?" This question came from Jack who had taken a seat at the table and lifted Amelia onto his lap.

"Always come back on Christmas Eve," Abe replied, glancing into the fireplace. "That's when Two Moons died givin' birth to our baby, so I come to the place where I last saw her purty face. Helps me remember how things were before she died."

"I'm sorry for your loss," Cynthia said sincerely.

Abe looked at her and gave a quick nod. All was quiet while Abe stoked the fire, watching as sparks went up the chimney.

"What about the baby?" Cynthia's mother asked breaking the silence. "Did he or she survive?"

Abe shook his head. "It grieves me to say it,

but both mother and son died on that Christmas Eve night."

"I too am sorry for your loss," Virginia said with feeling.

Abe nodded to the womenfolk. "It's bittersweet, but the good times Two Moons and I had together is what I hold on to."

"Whatcha got in there, mister?" Alan asked, pointing to the pack Abe had tossed on the floor.

Without saying a word, Abe picked up the pack, opened it, and pulled out a small object with a point on one end. "How'd ya like to have this?" He handed it to Alan.

"What is it?" Alan asked, turning the item over in his hand.

"It's an arrowhead," Abe replied. "The Injuns make 'em to put on their spears for hunting, spear fishing, and as a weapon to protect themselves."

Cynthia smiled as she watched Alan rub the arrowhead as though it were a piece of precious gold.

"Wow! Thanks!" Alan quickly put the carved stone in his pocket.

Abe reached into his pack and withdrew a string of colored beads. "Here's a purty necklace for ya," he said, slipping the beads over Amelia's head.

Amelia's eyes glistened as she looked up at Abe. "Thank you, Santa Claus."

Abe didn't argue with her this time—just smiled and patted her head. "I hafta say, the place hasn't felt this homey since my wife died," he said, gazing around the decorated room. "It needed a woman's touch." Abe grew quiet, looking toward the fire as though lost in memories from long ago. He looked back at them and said, "Guess I should be thankin'

you folks for makin' this Christmas a little less lonely for me."

Cynthia felt that Abe showing up when he did was a miracle of sorts. Seeing him and believing he was Santa Claus was just what Amelia needed to get her speaking again. And the fact that Abe carried in his pack two items any child would be intrigued with made Cynthia think God must have planned it all to give Jack's children a special Christmas Eve. She just hoped Abe would allow them to continue staying in his cabin, for they'd never survive the harsh winter in their wagons.

Chapter 11

Dear Diary,
*   Today as we celebrate Christmas,*
everyone is relieved that Abe has allowed
us to stay here in his cabin. Not only did he
give Alan and Amelia those items from his
wife's tribe, but he brought food with him—
enough to get us by until he or one of the
other men is able to get fresh meat again.

Abe seemed upset that we were here at first, but his attitude softened and he's agreed to let us stay until we're able to travel again. How I thank God for that. I think all of us being here, especially over Christmas, has helped Abe too and that warms my heart.

This morning Virginia and I gave the children the gifts we had for them. Alan and Amelia were excited and were also pleased with their father's gifts. Jack said the best Christmas present he could have received was to have his daughter laughing and talking again. Being trapped in the mountains has been frightening, but finding this cabin and experiencing Abe's generosity are truly answers to prayer. I'm confident that once the weather improves God will take us safely to California.

The only part I am dreading is becoming Walter's wife. How can I live the rest of my life with a man I don't love? If only there was a way Mama and I could make it on our own without relying on Walter to provide for our needs. I know I should be grateful and quit wishing for the impossible, but my selfish desires seem to keep creeping in. I pray every night that God will help me accept my plight and be a good wife.

I must close and help Mama and Virginia prepare our Christmas dinner. Thanks to Abe's hunting skills, a wild turkey is roasting in the fireplace. My mouth is already watering as the delicious aroma wafts through the cabin. Virginia used the last of her flour to bake two pies with some dried huckleberries Abe brought back to the cabin, so we're in for a special treat.

"Looks like you're workin' up a pretty good sweat," Jack said as Cole chopped some firewood from the big tree that fell. "Don't ya think we have enough already?"

"We can always use more." Cole paused a moment to wipe his wet forehead and started chopping again, as vigorously as before. "Who knows what the weather will bring in the next few days? It's best to get the rest of this tree cut and stacked close to the cabin where we can get our firewood easily."

"That makes sense, but you're not upset about anything are you?" Jack asked.

"What makes ya think I'm upset?"

"You've been sorta moody this morning, and you're attacking that wood like there's no tomorrow."

Cole set the ax aside and drew in a couple of deep breaths. He glanced toward the cabin

before he answered. "To tell ya the truth, I am kinda upset."

"About what?"

"Cynthia."

Jack quirked an eyebrow. "Did she say or do something you didn't like?"

Cole shook his head. "It's not that. It's just..." He stopped talking and motioned toward Walter who had come outside and was heading toward his wagon. "That guy really bothers me, and I don't understand what she sees in him."

"I don't either, but then it's not my place to be sayin' anything about who Cynthia marries."

Cole gritted his teeth. "She's too sweet for an old sourpuss like Walter, not to mention that she's a lot younger than him. I think he's using her, but I'm not sure for what."

"That may be true, but it's her decision, and I don't think she'd have agreed to marry him if

she didn't want to."

"You're probably right. I just wish. . ." Cole's voice trailed off. He'd most likely said more than he should.

Jack moved closer to Cole. "You're in love with her, aren't you? Don't deny it either. I can see it written all over your face."

Cole shrugged his shoulders. "Don't matter what I feel one way or the other. She's gonna marry Walter, and that's all there is to it."

Cynthia was about to help Virginia set the table when Walter reentered the cabin. He was really getting on her nerves, especially today, watching him sit around most of the morning while the rest of them hustled about making preparations for a nice Christmas Day. She'd been glad when he'd finally gone outside, but frowned seeing him back inside already.

Walter paused near the door, watching Cynthia a few minutes. Then he stepped up to her and said, "I need to speak to you about something. Will you take a walk with me outside?"

"Now?" she asked. *This makes no sense. Walter was just outside. Why didn't he ask me to go out with him then?* "Can't it wait until after we eat? I'm busy right now, helping to get things ready."

"I won't take but a few minutes," he said. "I need to talk to you alone."

"It's all right," Cynthia's mother interjected, shooing Cynthia away after glancing briefly at Walter. "I'll finish setting the table for you."

Cynthia couldn't imagine what was so important that it couldn't wait until they'd eaten their Christmas dinner, but wanting to avoid an argument, she slipped her bonnet on her head and wrapped a heavy woolen shawl around her

shoulders then followed Walter out the door.

I hope this doesn't take too long, she thought. She didn't want anything to spoil the day— something she knew Walter was capable of doing in just a matter of seconds.

Once outside, he took her arm and they walked toward his wagon. Pausing near the back of the wagon, he cleared his throat and said, "Your mother and I will be getting married when we reach California."

"What was that?" Cynthia asked, thinking she must have misunderstood.

"I am sure this must come as a shock to you, but Mable has agreed to become my wife."

Cynthia's mouth dropped open.

"Over the past few weeks, I have come to realize that Mable would be a better choice for me." A muscle on the side of Walter's cheek twitched. "The truth is, Cynthia, you're simply

too immature for me."

Her forehead creased. "You really think that?"

"Yes, I do."

"Then why did you try to kiss me recently?"

"It was a test. To see if my feelings for you were stronger than I'd thought."

Cynthia's jaw clenched. The idea that Walter would need to test his feelings for her by a mere kiss made her angry. And the fact that he saw her as immature only added to her irritation. And while she was relieved he no longer wanted to marry her, she couldn't believe Walter had asked Mama to marry him. It made no sense at all.

"What does my mother have to say about this?" Cynthia asked, challenging Walter with her eyes.

"She's agreeable to it."

Cynthia stared at Walter in disbelief. Never had she expected such a turn of events. "I—I don't believe you. What would make Mama agree to this?"

"I think it would be best if you asked her that yourself." He leaned against the wagon with a smug expression.

"Yes, I certainly will." Cynthia pulled her shawl tighter and turned to leave, but he stopped her by placing his hand on her shoulder.

"There's one more thing," Walter said.

She turned back around. "What's that?"

"I want you to know that as my future stepdaughter, I will provide for your needs."

"There's no reason for that," Cynthia said with a huff. "I can make my own way." She pivoted around and hurried toward the cabin, anxious to speak to her mother and get this resolved. *The nerve of that man, trying to keep a hold on me! And now as his stepdaughter—no!*

Chapter 12

Cynthia rushed into the cabin but realized right away that this wasn't a good time to talk with her mother as dinner was ready to serve. Their talk would have to wait.

Soon everyone gathered around the table, and after Jack offered a blessing, they ate and visited. The whole time, Cynthia kept glancing

at Walter and Mama to see if they might say something about their future plans, but neither said a word.

Maybe Walter made the whole thing up, she told herself. After all, she'd never seen much interaction between her mother and Walter except the usual conversation. *Of course, I have no idea what Walter may have said to Mama when I was out walking or spending time with Jack's children. When we reach California, he might be planning to discard me and Mama like pieces of unusable luggage. Maybe after traveling all this way with two women in his wagon, Walter's decided he doesn't need a wife telling him what to do. But what if Walter was telling the truth when he said Mama had agreed to marry him? Where will that leave me when we reach our destination? I wouldn't feel right about taking any charity from him.*

"You're awfully quiet, Cynthia," Mama said, pulling Cynthia out of her musings. "Don't you care for the delicious turkey that has miraculously graced our table today?"

Cynthia blinked several times. "Uh, yes, it's delicious. I was just thinking."

"About what?" Cole asked, looking at Cynthia strangely.

She smiled and said, "Oh, how grateful I am for this good meal and being able to spend Christmas in the warmth of this cabin with the friends I've made on our journey."

"We've all become friends," Virginia said, reaching over and giving Cynthia's arm a gentle squeeze. "When we first began this journey, we were strangers, but working together and helping each other through each trial that's come our way has strengthened us as people and given us a better understanding of each other."

All heads bobbed, except for Walter's. He sat quietly eating the food set before him.

Maybe he doesn't see any of us as friends, Cynthia thought. *He probably thinks we're all beneath him.* She was glad Walter was no longer interested in marrying her, but if he had somehow talked Mama into becoming his wife, he would be her stepfather. *I will not have that man thinking he can tell me what to do.*

Her appetite gone and her head pounding, Cynthia pushed her chair away from the table and stood.

"Where are you going?" Mama called as Cynthia grabbed her shawl and headed for the door.

"I—I need a bit of fresh air."

Cynthia had no more than gone out the door when it opened again, and Mama stepped out behind her. "Are you all right?" she asked.

"You're not feeling ill, I hope."

Cynthia shook her head. "I'm upset about something Walter told me earlier."

Mama stepped forward and placed her hand on Cynthia's arm. "Was it about me agreeing to marry him?"

Cynthia swallowed hard. "Is it true, Mama? Did you tell Walter you would become his wife?"

Mama nodded.

"When did this happen?"

"During the time you've spent with Jack's children, Walter and I have done a lot of talking. And since being here at the cabin, we've reached an agreement." Mama rubbed her hands briskly over her arms, obviously trying to warm them against the cold. "When Walter informed me that he didn't think you were the right woman for him, I nearly panicked, knowing how much we needed him. But then Walter surprised me

by saying that he thought he and I should be married, and that I would make him a better wife. So after talking about it some more, I agreed to marry him."

"I never saw this coming, and I surely can't let you make that sacrifice," Cynthia said, shaking her head. "I don't believe you love Walter any more than I do."

"It's not about love," Mama said. "It's about financial security and companionship, and Walter can offer me both."

"But he's several years younger than you, Mama, and he's not a very nice man."

"I'll admit, he does have some irritating ways, but he's smart and rich, and. . ."

"Did you make this decision for your sake or mine?" Cynthia asked.

"Both. I knew you didn't love Walter, but we still need his financial support, so I figured it

would be better if I married him, leaving you free to marry the man of your choice. Besides, I think Walter and I will get along quite well together. We both know what it takes to run a business, although my boarding home was small by comparison. Still, Walter and I have a lot of other things in common that involve the finer things in life."

Cynthia couldn't argue with that. Ever since she was a girl, she'd known that her mother fit better with high society ladies than some of the more down-to-earth, common women who'd attended their church in New York. "Are you absolutely sure that marrying Walter is the right thing to do?" she questioned.

"Yes," Mama replied.

Cynthia gave her mother a hug. "If that's what you want, then I wish you and Walter well. But I want you to know that when we get

to California I plan to look for a job. There is no way I will let Walter provide for me as his stepdaughter."

Mama patted Cynthia's arm. "Let's not talk about that right now. I think we should get back inside where it's warm and finish that good meal we took all morning to prepare." She giggled. "The way Abe was eating, there may not be much left."

"You go ahead," Cynthia said. "I want to stay out here awhile longer."

"But it's cold, and looks like it might start snowing again," Mama argued.

"I'll be fine. If I get chilled, I will come back inside. Right now I don't feel like eating."

Mama hesitated, but then she turned and headed back to the cabin.

Cynthia released a deep sigh. If Mama was determined to marry Walter, there wasn't much

she could do about it. She needed to pray about her own situation and give it time to sink in.

Cole waited until everyone was finished eating; then he mentioned that they needed more firewood and would head outside to get it.

"I'll get it!" Jack jumped up, put on his jacket, and hurried out the door before Cole could say another word.

So much for getting a chance to speak with Cynthia alone, Cole thought. She'd acted strangely during dinner, and he wanted to find out if something was wrong. If he worked up the nerve, he might have a talk with her about Walter—see if he could persuade Cynthia to break her engagement to Mr. Fancy Pants and agree to marry him. Of course that was probably a dumb idea, because a refined lady like her probably wouldn't want to be married to

a blacksmith who was going on a quest for gold. But if he didn't ask, he'd never know whether he had even the slightest chance with Cynthia, the first woman to capture his heart.

Cole gulped down the cup of coffee his sister offered him. Then, using the excuse that someone should help Jack get more firewood, he put on his jacket and went out the door.

When Cole stepped into the snow-covered yard, he was surprised to see Jack standing beside his wagon next to Cynthia. What surprised Cole even more was seeing them embracing. "That's just great," he mumbled, kicking a hunk of ice under his boot. *Shoulda known if she was gonna pick anyone it would have to be Jack. Guess he's better suited to her than me, and I know she really likes his kids. May as well take it like a man and give 'em my best wishes.*

As Cole approached Jack's wagon, the couple

broke their embrace and whirled around to look at Cole with surprised expressions.

"Oh Cole, you startled me," Cynthia said.

Jack nodded. "Same here. Didn't hear ya come out, I guess."

"No, don't suppose you did." Cole's irritation mounted. "Looked to me like you two were pretty busy when I came outside." He looked Jack in the eyes. "Thought ya said you had no romantic interest in Cynthia, and that you believed I oughta keep my feelings for her quiet 'cause she was promised to Walter."

"Never said that exactly," Jack replied. "Just said—"

"I'm not going to marry Walter," Cynthia spoke up.

"Y–you're not?" Cole stammered. If he weren't so upset with seeing Jack and Cynthia together, he'd have leapt for joy.

She shook her head. "Walter thinks I'm too immature for him, and he's decided to marry my mother instead."

Cole bit his lip to keep from laughing out loud. He couldn't imagine Mr. Fancy Pants married to Mable Cooper any more than he could her daughter. "Your mother agreed to this?" he asked, looking at Cynthia with raised brows.

She nodded. "And for your information, Jack was only hugging me because I gave him some advice."

Cole's eyes narrowed. "What kind of advice?"

"She was advising me to admit to your sister that I've come to care for her," Jack said.

Cole blinked a couple of times. "You're in love with Ginny?"

"That's right. I just haven't worked up the nerve to tell her yet." Jack raked his fingers through the ends of his thick hair. "I'm afraid

she might not return my feelings."

Cole thumped Jack's back. "If I know Ginny like I think I do, I've got a hunch she's smitten with you too."

"Do ya think so?" A wide smiled stretched across Jack's face. "Think I'll go inside and see if Virginia would like to take a walk with me."

Cole grinned. "That's the best idea you've had all day."

As Jack headed for the cabin, Cole drew in a deep breath then cleared his throat. If he was going to talk to Cynthia, it had to be now, because with them all being cooped up in the cabin like they were, he may not have another chance to tell her the way he felt. "Umm. . .Cynthia, there's somethin' I'd like to say."

"What's that?" she asked, smiling up at him.

"It's not snowing right now," he said, feeling suddenly tongue-tied.

She gave a slow nod, looking across the land. "I've noticed."

Cole jammed his hands in his pockets and rocked back and forth on his heels.

"Is something troubling you?" Cynthia inquired.

"Yes. No. Well, you see. . . The thing is. . . I'm in love with you, Cynthia, but I've kept my feelings hidden 'cause I knew you were promised to Walter, and I didn't know if you felt anything for me."

Cynthia tilted her head back and gazed at Cole in such a way that it made his toes curl inside his cold boots. "I do care for you, Cole. Very much, in fact. But until a few hours ago, when Walter revealed his plans to marry Mama, I wasn't free to even dream of a relationship with another man, let alone express the way I feel."

As the snow began to fall, Cole lifted

Cynthia's chin and kissed her gently on the lips. "I don't have much to offer, and there's no guarantee that I'll make it rich searching for gold, but when we get to California, would you do me the honor of becoming my wife?"

She nodded slowly, tears welling in her pretty eyes. "I'd like that very much." Cynthia sighed and leaned her head against his chest. "What a wonderful day this has been. My Christmas prayer was answered in more ways than one."

Epilogue

One year later

Dear Diary,

Cole and I found out that we're expecting a baby. What a joyous way to celebrate Christmas, knowing that next year at this time we'll have the laughter of a child filling our humble home here in Northern California.

Cole's plan of getting rich in the gold fields didn't pan out as he'd planned, but he made enough money to open a blacksmith's shop and build us a small home. The spirit of adventure we both felt when we first came here is still with us, only our focus is not on making money, but enjoying one another, helping others, and worshiping God, who has blessed us immeasurably.

I saw Mama the other day, and she seems happy being married to Walter. It didn't take him long to get a general store going, and more recently he's opened a hotel with a restaurant. Mama stays busy helping Walter at the hotel and hosting various social events.

Last week I received a letter from Virginia. Jack is busy helping his brother with the cattle ranch, and Virginia's time

*is taken up caring for Amelia and Alan.
She said Alan can't wait until he's bigger
and can go on cattle drives with his dad
and uncle Dan. Virginia's also teaching at
the one-room schoolhouse not far from their
home. She sounds happy and has settled
into her life as a cattle rancher's wife.*

*The mountain man, Abe, whose cabin
we stayed in last year, came to see us this fall.
We invited him to stay, but he said his place
is with his wife's Shoshone tribe, and that
he won't be going back to his cabin to live
again. He will check it from time to time
and leave the place stocked with supplies that
might be helpful to any other pioneers who
may need a shelter during a storm.*

Cynthia stopped writing and placed her
hand against her stomach. She felt such peace.

It was hard to believe that just a year ago things were so uncertain.

Thank You, Lord, for answering my prayers— not just at Christmas, but every day of the year.

RECIPES

Cynthia's Fried Apples

Without peeling, quarter as many tart apples as you would like. Lay apples close together, skin side down, in frying pan with salt pork fat or butter. Cover until well steamed then uncover and brown both sides, turning and watching closely to prevent burning.

Virginia's Spiced Venison

Fry three or four small slices of pork until light brown; then put in the raw venison steaks or roast. Let it brown a little on both sides then cover with water and stew over a moderate fire for 5 to 6 hours. Add water as it boils away so there will be enough left when done to make gravy. About half an hour before it's done, salt to taste and add 1 teaspoon whole allspice and a good sized cinnamon stick. When done, take out meat and thicken gravy with a little flour smoothed in water.

Mable's Fried Potatoes

Peel raw potatoes then cut into thin rings or into one continuous shaving. Put potatoes in cold water until you have enough to cook then drain on a cloth. Fry potatoes quickly in plenty of hot fat and sprinkle with salt and pepper. Once cooked, dry them well from the grease and sprinkle with salt. Potatoes may also be fried with onions and served as an accompaniment to meat.

ABOUT THE AUTHOR

New York Times bestselling and award-winning author Wanda E. Brunstetter is one of the founders of the Amish fiction genre. She has written close to 90 books translated in four languages. With over 10 million copies sold, Wanda's stories consistently earn spots on the nation's most prestigious bestseller lists and have received numerous awards.

Wanda enjoys photography, ventriloquism, gardening, bird-watching, beachcombing, and spending time with her family. She and her husband, Richard, have been blessed with two grown children, six grandchildren, and two great-grandchildren.

To learn more about Wanda, visit her website at www.wandabrunstetter.com.

Enjoy More Christmas
from Wanda E. Brunstetter!

The Lopsided Christmas Cake

Grab This Re-Release Before It's Gone!

A baking flop still manages to earn high bids from admiring bachelors at an Amish charity auction when twin sisters Elma and Thelma Hochstetler recreate their grandmother's Christmas cake recipe in front of a live audience. Will the highest bidder also win a sister's heart?

Paperback / 978-1-68322-728-1 / $6.99